›THE RED HEELS‹

ROBERT D. SAN SOUCI

PICTURES BY GARY KELLEY

Dial Books *New York*

Published by Dial Books
A Division of Penguin Books USA Inc.
375 Hudson Street
New York, New York 10014

Text copyright © 1996 by Robert D. San Souci
Pictures copyright © 1996 by Gary Kelley
All rights reserved
Designed by Atha Tehon
Printed in the U.S.A.
First Edition
1 3 5 7 9 10 8 6 4 2

Library of Congress Cataloging in Publication Data
San Souci, Robert D.
The red heels / Robert D. San Souci ; pictures by Gary Kelley.
p.   cm.
Summary: An itinerant shoemaker in colonial New England makes a pair of shoes for
a beautiful young woman, although he fears the red heels are a sign that she is a witch.
ISBN 0-8037-1133-6 (trade). — ISBN 0-8037-1134-4 (library)
[1. Shoes—Fiction. 2. Witches—Fiction.] I. Kelley, Gary, ill. II. Title.
PZ7.S1947Re 1996 [E]—dc20 91-22532 CIP AC

*The full-color artwork was prepared with pastels on paper. It was then
color-separated and reproduced in red, yellow, blue, and black halftones.*

For Ellen and Eric . . .
Like Diamonds in the Sky!

R.S.S.

To Cydney and Kyle

G.K.

Jonathan Dowse was a shoemaker in colonial New England. A young man, he traveled the country roads, carrying his small workbench, tool kit, and supply of leather on his back. When he found a family that needed his services, he would stay until everyone had new shoes.

Hunched over his bench near the kitchen fire, he would chat with the goodwife at her spinning during the day, and with the farmer puffing his pipe in the evening.

The children watched spellbound as he traced the outline of their feet on leather that had been soaked in a pail of water until it was soft. This he cut to proper shape and size. Then Jonathan sewed the shoes with waxed linen thread tied 'round a hog's bristle needle, and pulled through holes he had bored with his awl. Often he let the eager children try a stitch or two, then deftly finished the job himself.

One autumn afternoon as he stored his knives and hammer, beeswax and thread in his kit, the farmwife whose shoes he had just finished said, "Tarry this evening, Master Jonathan, and tell us more about Plymouth and Boston."

"Alas, I must make my way north to Indian Cove," the shoemaker said, folding up his leather apron. "That town has many feet waiting to be shod."

When she could not change his mind, the good woman said, "Have a care that thou pass through the woods before dark. Strange things have happened there when the sun is gone."

Jonathan thanked her for her concern and for the journey-cake she gave him to eat along the way. Bidding the family farewell, he set off.

The day was cool but bright. Jonathan sang to himself as he walked the lonely path through the forest. After a time he paused to eat the journey-cake, his back to a sun-warmed stone. Thinking that he would close his eyes for just a moment, he fell asleep.

When he awoke, it was late in the day. The woods, which had been filled with birds' songs and the hum of insects, had grown hushed. Jonathan thought of the goodwife's warning, and hurried on his way.

The path forked and forked again, becoming many paths. In the last light of day Jonathan realized he was lost. All around him he heard moans and whispers and hisses.

Then through the dangerous dark he spotted the welcome glow of candles. Soon he came to a tidy cottage of hand-hewn oak in a clearing. Smoke drifted up from a fieldstone chimney. Light poured out through the diamond-shaped panes in the windows on each side of the door.

Jonathan knocked at the door, which was opened by a handsome young woman. Her dark hair was gathered under a prim white cap. She folded her hands across the waist of her white starched apron and studied him with sharp green eyes.

"Who art thou, sir?" she asked.

"Jonathan Dowse, mistress," he answered. "An honest cobbler who has lost his way."

"Come in," she invited. "Thou must do no more traveling this night. Wolves and worse prowl the woods."

She showed him into a large room, and sat him on a high-backed chair beside a blazing fireplace, as wide and deep as a cave. The air was spiced with the scent of burning pinewood.

She brought him bean porridge, brown bread, and tea. He learned that her name was Rebecca Wyse, but little else. While he ate, she busied herself with mending. Staring at the woman sitting across from him—as fine and fair as any he had ever set eyes on—Jonathan felt the stirrings of love.

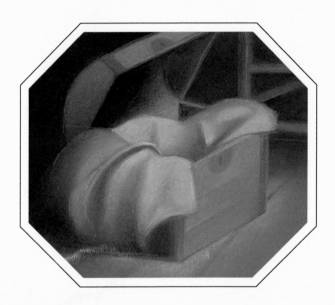

When he had finished his meal, he said, "Perhaps I can offer thee my services as a shoemaker to pay for this welcome food and shelter."

"Indeed, thou can do just that!" she said with a pleased smile. From a wooden chest she pulled out a pair of dainty, but over-worn shoes with creased and cracked leather. Curiously the carved wooden heels, painted with red lacquer, seemed brand-new. "These heels are sturdy, but cry out to be affixed to new shoes."

Jonathan nodded, but the sight caused him dismay. He had often heard country goodwives say that such red heels were the sign of a witch.

But Rebecca spoke so gently and smiled so charmingly that he put aside his fear of the antique shoes. Weary from his journey, he promised, "Tomorrow I will make thee a fine new pair of shoes."

"That would please me very much," Rebecca said. "These shoes belonged to my mother, and the heels belonged to her mother before her."

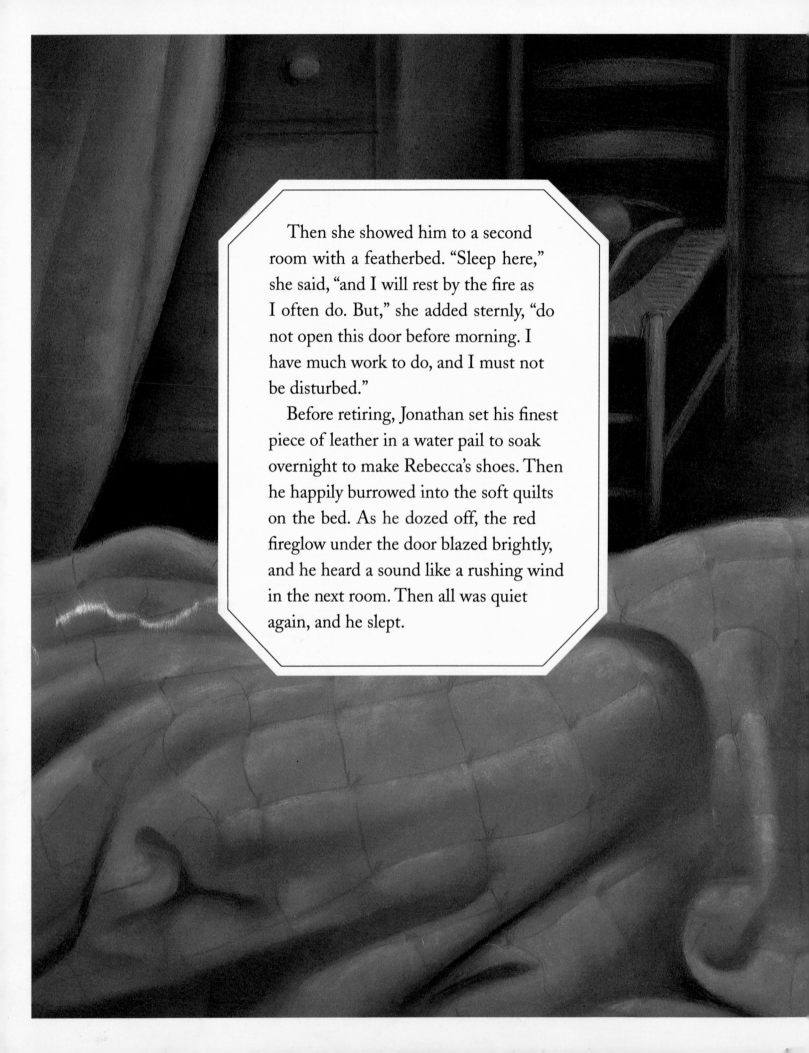

Then she showed him to a second room with a featherbed. "Sleep here," she said, "and I will rest by the fire as I often do. But," she added sternly, "do not open this door before morning. I have much work to do, and I must not be disturbed."

Before retiring, Jonathan set his finest piece of leather in a water pail to soak overnight to make Rebecca's shoes. Then he happily burrowed into the soft quilts on the bed. As he dozed off, the red fireglow under the door blazed brightly, and he heard a sound like a rushing wind in the next room. Then all was quiet again, and he slept.

In the morning he took the leather out of the pail, and set to work to make a pair of shoes worthy of the fine red heels and their beautiful owner. He carefully measured Rebecca's foot, cut the softened leather, and stitched it with the utmost nicety.

While he worked, Rebecca began to peel some apples for a pie she was making. Watching her, Jonathan daydreamed that he would one day marry Rebecca and buy a shop in town. There he would fashion fine shoes for his neighbors, while Rebecca kept his accounts and tended their children.

Sighing, he put his dreams aside and gave full attention to his work.

At day's end, while Rebecca watched eagerly, Jonathan removed the red lacquer heels from her worn-out shoes and cobbled them to the new pair. At last he presented the finished shoes to her.

Delighted, she clutched them to her heart and danced around the room, crying, "They are a wonder, Master Jonathan! They are the finest shoes in the colonies!"

Her joy and her praise fanned the love-fire in Jonathan's heart. But for all her happiness she seemed impatient for him to be off to bed and to be by herself. Setting the shoes on a wooden chest, she served a simple meal of hasty pudding—cornmeal mush and milk—and boiled vegetables.

Jonathan's eyes and fingers were sore from his labors, and his heart was pained by Rebecca's unwillingness to talk with him, so he went to bed.

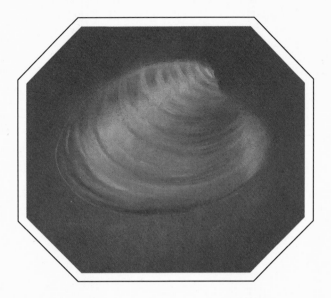

He shut the door; but he could not sleep. When the firelight blazed redly under the door as it had the night before, he climbed out of bed and put his eye to the crack between door and frame. He saw Rebecca put on her new red-heeled shoes. Then she took a quahog shell from a bowl of them on the ledge above the hearth, where the fire had sunk to embers.

As Jonathan watched, the woman scratched behind each ear with the clamshell, saying, "Whisk! Whusk!"

To Jonathan's astonishment, she flew up the chimney with a sound like roaring wind.

The shoemaker ran into the room and took another shell from the bowl. Then he scratched behind his ears, just as Rebecca had done. "Whisk! Whusk!" he cried.

Instantly he shot up the chimney and flew over treetops, until he landed in a heap beside a forest pond.

Brushing himself off, he saw Rebecca dancing on the surface of the moonlit pond, as if it were a plate of solid silver. Around and around she whirled— her new shoes outlined in thin white flames, her red heels glowing like coals. She leapt lightly from ripple to ripple, as if she weighed no more than an eiderdown feather.

When she spotted Jonathan, she laughed and danced over to him.

"Thou hast discovered my secret delight," she said, "to come and dance beneath the moon. But thou must promise never to betray my secret."

"I swear to thee, I will not," he said.

"Then, sir, will thou come and dance with me?" she asked, reaching out her hands to Jonathan. "Thou hast given me the most wonderful dancing shoes ever."

Poor Jonathan was torn between his fear of witchery and his love for the beautiful young woman. At last love won over fear, and he stretched out his hands to Rebecca.

Then they spun together, like skaters on ice, across the moon-silvered surface of the pond.

"Thou put some new magic in these shoes of mine!" she said. "Did thy leather come from a dragon's wing?"

"'Tis merely good calfskin—my best and no better, though it seems hardly worthy of thee," said Jonathan, blushing.

"Then surely thou must be a wizard," she teased, "and whispered some spell over thy hammer and needle."

"My only spell is the skill I possess," Jonathan replied, "and good honest work." In his heart he knew that love had been mixed in with his handiwork. But he dared not say this to her.

"So thy magic must stay a mystery," she decided. Then she warned him, "Hold tight to my hands, upon peril of thy life!"

Jonathan did as she said.

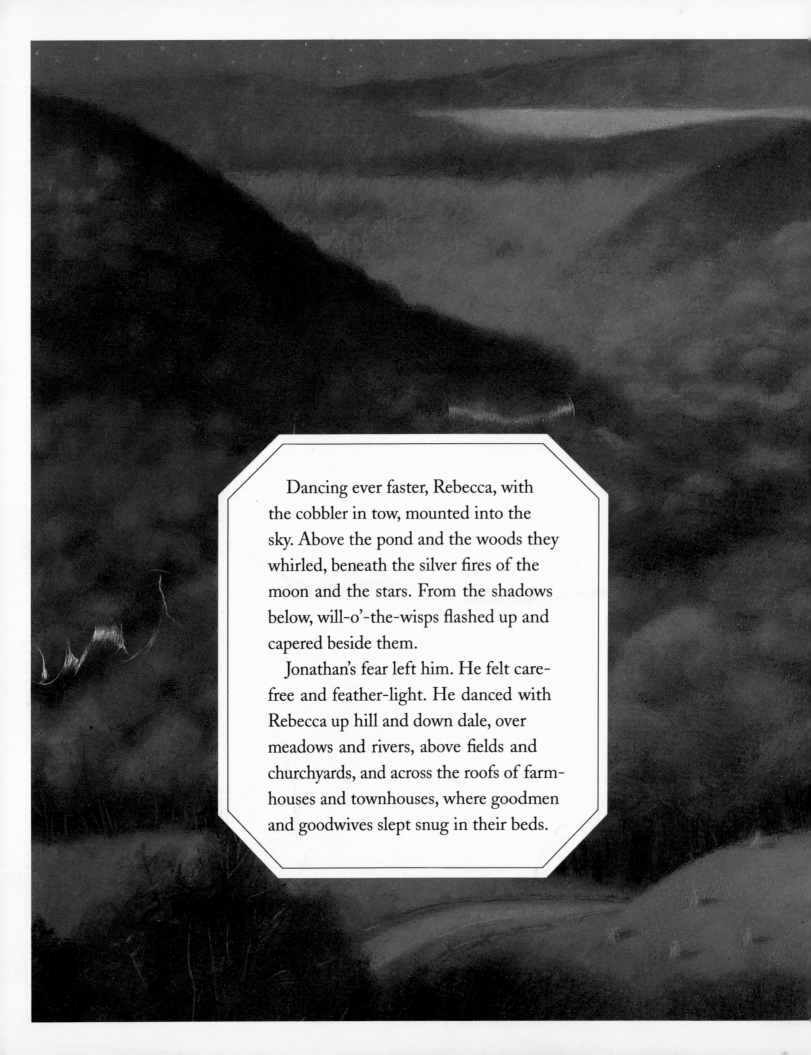

Dancing ever faster, Rebecca, with the cobbler in tow, mounted into the sky. Above the pond and the woods they whirled, beneath the silver fires of the moon and the stars. From the shadows below, will-o'-the-wisps flashed up and capered beside them.

Jonathan's fear left him. He felt care-free and feather-light. He danced with Rebecca up hill and down dale, over meadows and rivers, above fields and churchyards, and across the roofs of farm-houses and townhouses, where goodmen and goodwives slept snug in their beds.

At the first sign of dawn Rebecca drew them back to the pond. They descended through the night air as easily as if they were skipping down stairs.

When they stood on the shore, she said, "Do as I do." From the pocket of her apron she took her clamshell, scratched behind each ear, and said, "Whusk! Whisk!"

Away into the brightening sky she flew. Jonathan took his own shell, cried, "Whusk! Whisk!" and followed her.

In a moment he saw Rebecca's cottage below him. Then the two of them plunged down the chimney and once again stood before the hearth. The fire had gone to ash; soft morning light filled the room.

The airiness and excitement of the night drained out of Jonathan. He felt heavy and weary. "I must be on my way soon," he said, looking at his bench and kit.

But Rebecca said, "Tarry awhile, sleep, and we will dance again tonight. Thy shoes on my feet and thy hand in mine make a magic unlike any I have ever known."

At these words his spirit soared as if it were dancing in red-heeled shoes. He said to Rebecca, "Let me rest for a time, and I will squire thee gladly across the night sky."

So Jonathan remained at the little cottage in the forest. He chopped firewood and repaired the roof, while Rebecca went about her daily tasks. In the evening they would share a hasty meal. Then they would use their shells to transport themselves to the shores of the forest pond, where they danced upon water and over the treetops until daybreak.

But one afternoon Rebecca returned from an errand to find Jonathan sitting on his shoemaker's bench in front of the fireplace. His kit was open, and he was examining his cobbler's tools with pleasure and regret.

Jonathan said to Rebecca, "I cannot stay here any longer. I do not belong dancing across the sky, any more than thou belong in town helping a husband manage his shop. I miss the simple joys of my calling, the pleasure of shaping good leather into shoes. I miss talking with customers, and seeing their happiness when they put on the shoes I have made for them."

Sighing deeply, Jonathan told Rebecca, "I must continue on to Indian Cove before the winter snows arrive."

The tears in her green eyes almost melted his resolve. If she had said a single word, he would have remained. But she sat silently by the fire, mending a skirt, while he repacked his kit.

When he was ready, she pointed out the shortest way to Indian Cove. They touched hands briefly, then he set off. When he looked back to the cottage, her door was firmly shut.

Through the rest of the fall and winter Jonathan traveled the roads and lanes around Indian Cove. Word of his fine workmanship brought him plenty of business. But many a farmwife's soft voice or sweet smile brought Rebecca to mind. So he worked even harder to ease the sadness he felt. By spring he had saved enough money to buy a small shop in town.

Sitting at his bench whittling a shoe heel, he thought of Rebecca Wyse. On his lonely walks along the edge of the forest, the glimpse of a red-winged blackbird made him think of her red-heeled shoes. He often dreamed of a magic wood where a beautiful woman danced with will-o'-the-wisps beneath the moon.

But many a night, when the stars were out and the moon was high and the children were asleep in crib or trundle bed, Jonathan and Rebecca would put on their night shoes. They would take clamshells from a bowl on the mantel, scratch behind their ears, whisper, "Whisk! Whusk!" so as not to disturb the sleeping youngsters, and fly up the chimney.

Then they would dance between the moon and its reflection in the forest pond, until the sun came up or a restless child's night-cry summoned them back to hearth and home.